For William and Laurie Oakley—
from whom I inherited my first set of oil paints
and the keys to a magical world populated by knights, dragons, and unicorns

BESTIARY

NATVRALIS · HISTORIA

JONATHAN HUNT
BESTIARY
AN ILLUMINATED ALPHABET OF MEDIEVAL BEASTS

Simon & Schuster Books for Young Readers

PRONUNCIATION GUIDE

Bestiary	BESS-chee-air-ee or BEES-chee-air-ee or BESS-tee-air-ee
Amphisbaena	am-fis-BEE-nuh
Basilisk	BASS-uh-lisk or BAZZ-uh-lisk
Catoblepas	kuh-TAH-bluh-pas
Dog	DAWG or DOG
Echeneis	ek-uh-NAY-iss
Firedrake	FI-er-drayk
Griffin	GRIFF-un
Hippocampus	hip-uh-KAMP-us
Ichneumon	ick-NOO-man or ick-NYOO-man
Javelin Snake	JAV-uh-lun SNAKE
Karkadann	KAHR-kah-dan
K'i-lin	KEE-lin
Kirin	KEE-rin
Kraken	KRAHK-un
Leucrocuta	loo-kruh-KOT-uh
Manticore	MAN-tih-kore
Mi'raj	MEE-rahj
Nycticorax	nik-TIK-uh-raks
Ozaena	oh-ZEE-nuh
Phoenix	FEE-niks
Questing Beast	KWEST-ing BEEST
Roc	RAHK
Sphinx	SFINKS
Triton	TRY-tun
Unicorn	YOU-nuh-korn
Vegetable Lamb	VEJ-tuh-buhl LAM
Wyvern	WYE-vurn
Xanthus	ZAN-thus
Yale	YALE
Ziphius	ZIFF-ee-us

Amphisbaena

The word amphisbaena means *to go both ways*. This is appropriate, as the amphisbaena had a head on both ends of its reptilian body. If one head fell asleep, the other would remain awake. The amphisbaena could pursue victims who tried to run away by placing one head into the mouth of the other and rolling down the road like a hoop!

Basilisk ◉ If a seven-year-old cock laid a spherical, yolkless egg that was then hatched by a toad or a serpent, a basilisk was sure to emerge. ⟿ The fiery breath of the basilisk was so deadly that the land was laid waste for miles around, and the very glance of the basilisk was fatal. Travelers were advised to carry a mirror, for after one look at its own reflection the creature would drop dead.

Catoblepas ◇

The Ethiopian catoblepas had an enormous appetite and could never find enough food. It would often gnaw its own forelegs in frustration. The catoblepas could kill with a single look. 〰 Luckily, the creature was sluggish and had difficulty keeping its heavy head from bobbing and knocking against its chest. In fact, the catoblepas's name means *that which looks downward.* ◦

Dog 🛡 Ancient writers praised the dog's loyalty and intelligence, and statues of guard dogs were often carved at the feet of medieval tomb effigies. ✦ ✦ ✦ But there was also a menacing aspect to these normally faithful animals. The dreaded Black Dog of Ireland and Scotland stalked travelers on the moors. ✒ Those who heard its footfalls or gazed into its eyes were struck dumb with fear and soon withered away and died. 🌿 🌿 🌿 🌿 🌿 🌿 🌿 🌿

Echeneis ○ The echeneis was the bane of ancient sailors. Its name means *delay* or *hindrance*. A cartilaginous disk atop its flattened head acted as a suction cup. When a single echeneis attached itself to the Roman Emperor Caligula's ship, the combined might of four hundred oarsmen could not budge the vessel!

 **Firedrake** ✦ Firedrakes were native to the rugged lands of the north, where they jealously guarded their hoards of treasure. Beowulf, the hero of an Old English poem, fought a desperate battle against a firedrake and defeated the fire-breathing monster at the cost of his own life. His people cremated their king's body and buried his ashes with the firedrake's treasure in a barrow overlooking the sea.

Griffin The offspring of the eagle, monarch of the skies, and the lion, king of beasts, griffins were often included in the coats of arms of noble European families. Many griffins made their nests in the Caucasus Mountains. A griffin's feathers could cure blindness, and a drinking horn made from a griffin's claw would change color in the presence of poison.

 **Hippocampus** ～◇～ These untamed stallions and mares of the sea swam in herds in the waters from Norway to Brittany. ⤳ They avoided contact with humans, preferring to graze peaceably on the weeds and grasses that grew along the ocean floor. ⌒⌒⌒⌒⌒⌒⌒

Ichneumon

Ichneumons lived along the Nile River in Egypt. They hated serpents and crocodiles and never passed up an opportunity to attack either one. ▲▲▲▲▲▲▲ Often a crocodile would fall asleep on the riverbank with its mouth full of fish, attracting the trochilus bird, which would clean out the crocodile's mouth. While the huge jaws gaped wide, the ichneumon would dart down the crocodile's throat and gnaw out its belly.

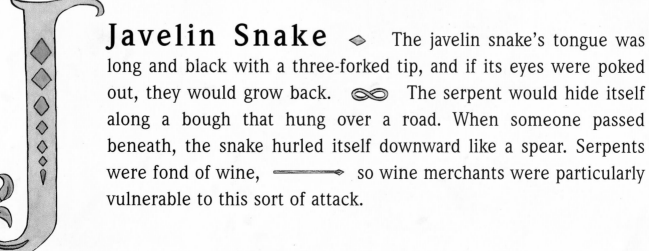

Javelin Snake

Javelin Snake ◇ The javelin snake's tongue was long and black with a three-forked tip, and if its eyes were poked out, they would grow back. ∞ The serpent would hide itself along a bough that hung over a road. When someone passed beneath, the snake hurled itself downward like a spear. Serpents were fond of wine, ——➤ so wine merchants were particularly vulnerable to this sort of attack.

 **Kraken** ◯ Of all the creatures that haunted the ocean depths, the kraken was the most feared by sailors. A kraken would spend thousands of years slumbering beneath the sea, ⌇⌇⌇ but when it rose up to crush a ship in its sucker-lined tentacles, no one lived to tell the tale. The monster was so large that a kraken floating on the surface was sometimes mistaken for an island. ∞

Leucrocuta  The leucrocuta of Africa could outrace a gazelle and swallow it down in two or three gulps, then chew the meal in its tooth-lined stomach. If just the shadow of a leucrocuta passed over a dog, the animal would be struck dumb with fear. The leucrocuta would sometimes call out in imitation of a human voice, and its victim, thinking that someone was in trouble, would rush straight into the creature's waiting jaws.

Manticore This monster's name came from the old Persian word for *man-eater*. The manticore had the body of a lion and a human face. It had triple rows of razor-sharp fangs, and a poisonous scorpionlike tail with spines that could be shot like darts at its prey. The manticore was said to possess a shrill voice like a small trumpet or pipe.

Nycticorax

The nycticorax and the pelican were natural enemies. The pelican was irresistibly drawn to the sun and would fly off daily in pursuit of it. The nycticorax would then descend upon the pelican's unattended chicks and kill them. Upon returning, the pelican would stab miserably at its own breast with the sharp tip of its beak. The flow of blood that dripped upon the chicks would miraculously revive them.

Ozaena

 Ozaena means *stink-polyp*. The creature was so named because of its offensive odor. Most ozaenas were small in size, and preferred to remain near the sea bottom. In rare instances, larger species of these polyps attacked swimmers and drowned them. One giant ozaena that terrorized a village in Spain had a head as large as a ninety-gallon cask, and tentacles thirty feet long!

Phoenix

The noble phoenix was admired the world over, even though the bird was wise enough to distance itself from human affairs. When the phoenix neared the end of its long life, it built a nest of sweet-smelling spices and gums at the top of a palm tree. At dawn, the phoenix would sing to the sun in its delicate voice and then clap its wings once, setting the nest and itself aflame. Before the ashes cooled, a newly formed phoenix burst forth from its parent's pyre.

Questing Beast

Questing Beast One day, when King Arthur stopped to rest by a spring, he was surprised by a sound like thirty baying hounds. A strange animal with a snake's head, the body of a leopard, the back legs of a lion, and the hooves of a deer burst through the underbrush, pursued by King Pellinore. Pellinore hunted the Questing Beast, as he called the creature, all his life, but he never managed to catch it.

 **Roc** ◆ These huge, eagle-shaped birds made their home on the isle of Madagascar, but they frequently raided mainland India and Africa for food. ◆ Adult rocs were known to carry off fully grown elephants! The European explorer Marco Polo related how a foreign envoy presented a roc feather as large as a palm frond to the Great Khan of Cathay. The khan was most impressed with this gift. ⌐⌐⌐

Sphinx  The word sphinx comes from a Greek root word meaning *strangler*. Sphinxes were known in Greece, Assyria, Persia, Phoenicia, and Egypt. After a day of hunting at Giza, the future Pharaoh Tuthmosis IV took a nap. In a dream he was told to clear away the sand from the spot where he slept. Upon awakening, Tuthmosis unearthed the statue of the Great Sphinx, which to this day sits looking east over the Nile valley.

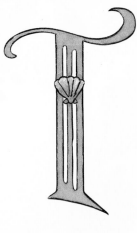 **Triton** Tritons were half-human, half-fish creatures with scales covering their torsos, fishlike tails, and sharp teeth and claws. They spent much of their time carousing, riding the wave tops, and blowing their conch shell trumpets. Tritons often changed their tails into legs so they could spend part of their long lives among humans.

Unicorn ● The snow-white, horselike beast depicted in tapestries and paintings of the European Middle Ages was just one kind of unicorn. ●●● There was also the dragonlike kirin of Japan, and the k'i-lin of China. From Persia came the foul-tempered karkadann and the mi'raj. A vicious carnivore, the mi'raj looked like a yellow hare with a black spiral horn growing from its forehead.

Vegetable Lamb ♣ The vegetable lamb

was prized for its soft, warm coat. When ripe, the small, woolly lamb would emerge from a pod to graze on the vegetation that surrounded the main stalk of its plant.

However, the lambs remained attached to their pods by a long stem, and once there was no longer any food within reach, the little creatures would starve. ♣

Wyvern ◇◇ The winged wyvern had many characteristics in common with its cousin the dragon. However, the wyvern had only two legs (dragons had four), and a barbed tail. ⟞══⟝ The wyvern's snakelike head and fangs show how its name may have developed from the Latin word for *viper*. Medieval knights were often called upon to defend people and cities from rampaging wyverns.

Xanthus ⬥

King Diomedes owned four flesh-eating mares that were so dangerous, he had to keep them chained up in stalls cast from bronze. Their names were Podargus, Lampon, Deinus, and Xanthus. The eighth labor of the Greek hero Hercules was to steal these mares. After a battle, Hercules defeated King Diomedes and fed him to his own monsters.

Yale

Yale Yales were bred in India to guard sacred temples. The two spiral horns that grew from the yale's head could be pointed in any direction, allowing it to fend off attackers from all sides. It could also use its curved tusks to dispatch enemies. The yale was often shown on heraldic crests and coats of arms.

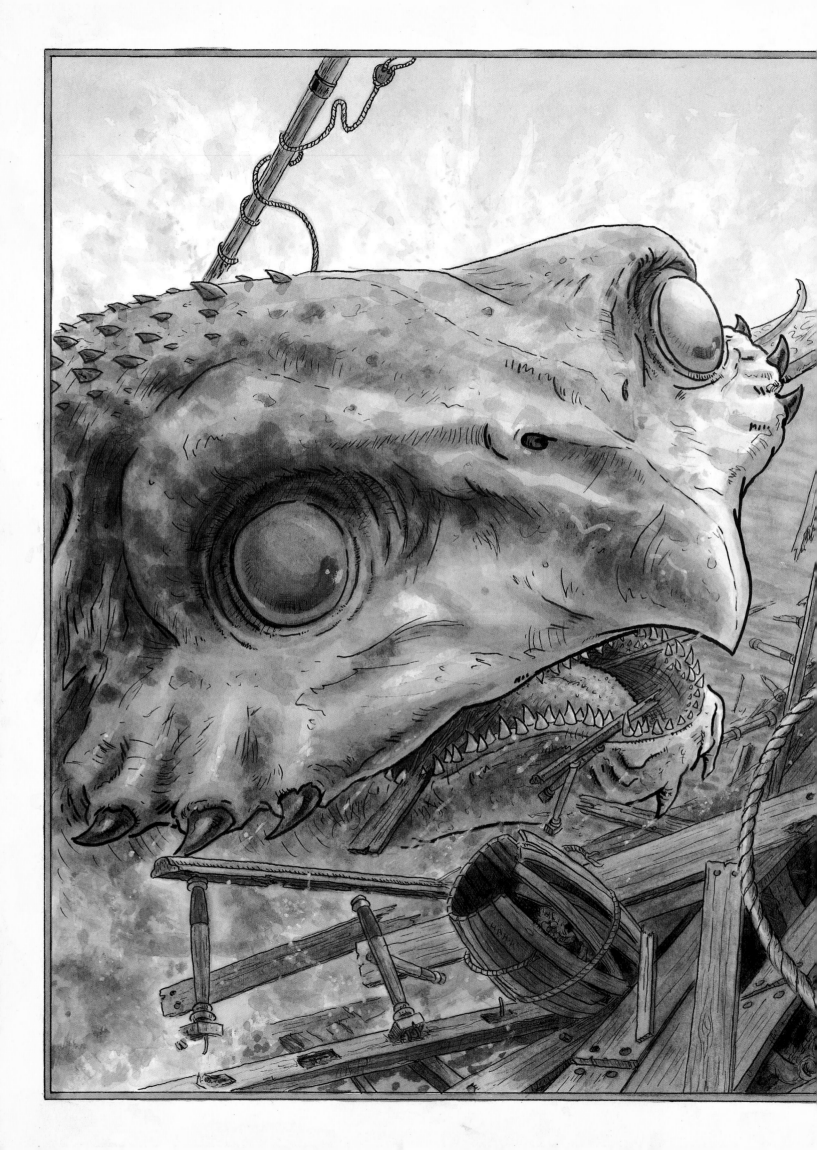

Ziphius ⬤ The ziphius, or water-owl, was a vicious predator of the sea. Larger than most whales, it attacked every ship it encountered. ～◡～ When it spotted a vessel on the surface, the ziphius would erupt out of the sea and come crashing down onto the craft. ～◉～ The last sight a terrified sailor would see was the lidless eyes rolling in their sockets and the snapping, wedge-shaped beak that framed its gaping mouth. ⟫⟫⟫⟫⟫⟫⟫⟫⟫⟫⟫⟫⟫⟫⟫⟫⟫⟫⟫⟫➤

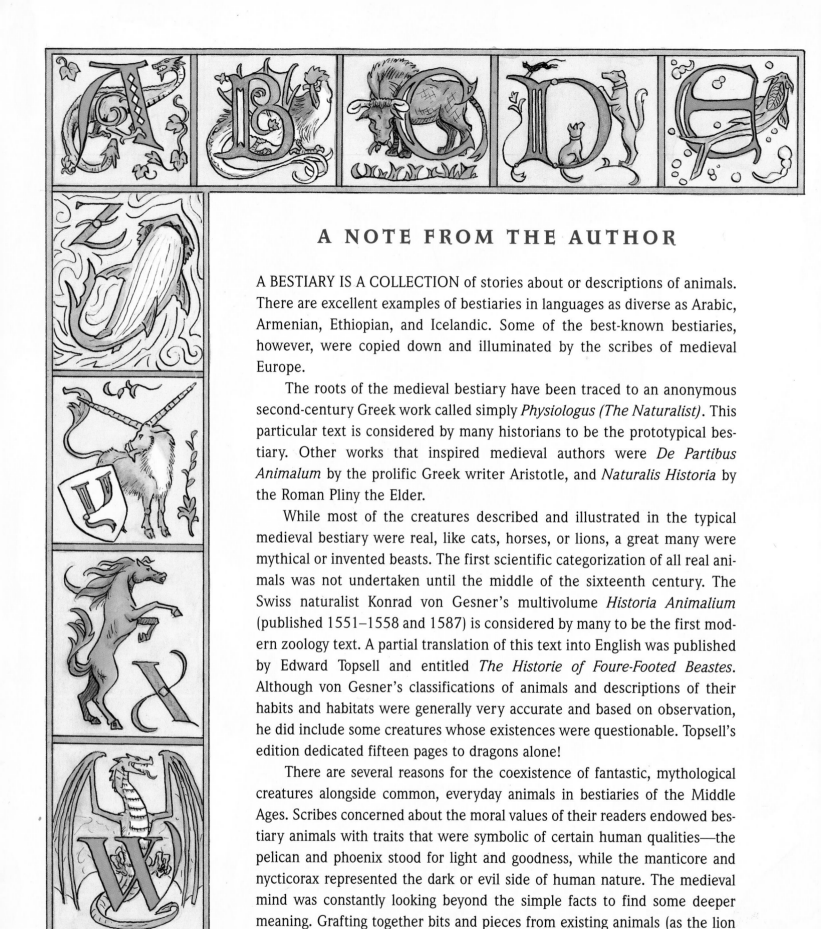

A NOTE FROM THE AUTHOR

A BESTIARY IS A COLLECTION of stories about or descriptions of animals. There are excellent examples of bestiaries in languages as diverse as Arabic, Armenian, Ethiopian, and Icelandic. Some of the best-known bestiaries, however, were copied down and illuminated by the scribes of medieval Europe.

The roots of the medieval bestiary have been traced to an anonymous second-century Greek work called simply *Physiologus (The Naturalist)*. This particular text is considered by many historians to be the prototypical bestiary. Other works that inspired medieval authors were *De Partibus Animalum* by the prolific Greek writer Aristotle, and *Naturalis Historia* by the Roman Pliny the Elder.

While most of the creatures described and illustrated in the typical medieval bestiary were real, like cats, horses, or lions, a great many were mythical or invented beasts. The first scientific categorization of all real animals was not undertaken until the middle of the sixteenth century. The Swiss naturalist Konrad von Gesner's multivolume *Historia Animalium* (published 1551–1558 and 1587) is considered by many to be the first modern zoology text. A partial translation of this text into English was published by Edward Topsell and entitled *The Historie of Foure-Footed Beastes*. Although von Gesner's classifications of animals and descriptions of their habits and habitats were generally very accurate and based on observation, he did include some creatures whose existences were questionable. Topsell's edition dedicated fifteen pages to dragons alone!

There are several reasons for the coexistence of fantastic, mythological creatures alongside common, everyday animals in bestiaries of the Middle Ages. Scribes concerned about the moral values of their readers endowed bestiary animals with traits that were symbolic of certain human qualities—the pelican and phoenix stood for light and goodness, while the manticore and nycticorax represented the dark or evil side of human nature. The medieval mind was constantly looking beyond the simple facts to find some deeper meaning. Grafting together bits and pieces from existing animals (as the lion

and the eagle were combined to create the griffin) gave the authors and artists of bestiaries an opportunity to expand this symbolism in new directions.

Another factor was the lack of swift and reliable transportation. If an unknown animal was killed in a distant land, there was no way to preserve the carcass in a recognizable state to be brought overland or by sea to its final destination. So artists and writers had to rely on highly embellished verbal descriptions of newly discovered creatures. Even artists who did manage to draw animals from nature were often hamstrung by having to present their subjects in the stylized and stiff manner dictated by popular taste, as well as by the lack of truly portable art materials. But probably the most common reason for the odd names or appearances of some bestiary animals was simply human error. There are many examples of confused or sloppily translated source materials, compounded by the scribe's boredom with the meticulous process of copying the text.

During the time of the Middle Ages, the world was an incredibly vast, mysterious, and often dangerous place. Much of the knowledge that we take for granted today was beyond the understanding of even the most advanced medieval scholars. Without the benefit of electric lights, the nights must have seemed very dark and filled with unimaginable terrors. If someone was to disappear without a trace, or die suddenly and unexpectedly of unknown causes, then it was perfectly acceptable to explain the unexplainable by blaming it on a monster. And who knows? Sometimes, just maybe, they were right.

—JONATHAN HUNT

ABOUT THE ART

The illustrations are rendered in ink, transparent watercolors, acrylics, and color pencils on 140 lb. hot-pressed watercolor paper. The decorated capitals, like the beasts themselves, are hybrids. The letters and dingbats are original designs created specifically for this book, based on classical Roman and medieval sources. The art was color-separated by laser scanner and reproduced using cyan, magenta, yellow, and black inks.

BIBLIOGRAPHY

Barlowe, Wayne. *Expedition*. New York: Workman Publishing Co., Inc. 1990.

Benton, Janetta Rebold. *The Medieval Menagerie: Animals in the Art of the Middle Ages*. New York: Abbeville Press Publishers, 1992.

Borges, Jorge Luis. *The Book of Imaginary Beings*. London: Cape, 1970.

Cohen, Daniel. *The Encyclopedia of Monsters*. New York: Dorset Press, 1989.

Day, David. *A Tolkien Bestiary*. New York: Ballantine Books, 1979.

Enchanted World: Magical Beasts, The. Alexandria, VA: Time-Life Books, 1985.

Fagg, Christopher. *Fabulous Beasts*. Windermere, FL: R. Rourke Publishing Co., 1981.

Froud, Brian, and Alan Lee. *Faeries*. New York: Abrams, 1978.

Guirand, Felix, ed., translated by Richard Aldington and Delano Ames. *New Larousse Encyclopedia of Mythology*. London: Hamlyn/Reed International Books Ltd., 1994.

Hargreaves, Joyce. *Hargreaves New Illustrated Bestiary*. Great Britain: Gothic Image Publications, 1990.

Hogarth, Peter, and Val Clery. *Dragons*. New York: Viking Press, 1979.

Huber, Richard. *Treasury of Fantastic and Mythological Creatures: 1,087 Renderings from Historic Sources*. New York: Dover Publications, Inc., 1981.

Huygen, Wil, and Rien Poortvliet. *Gnomes*. New York: H. N. Abrams, 1977.

Lang, Andrew, ed. *King Arthur: Tales of the Round Table*. New York: Schocken Books, 1976 (first published 1902).

Leach, Maria, ed. *Funk & Wagnalls Standard Dictionary of Folklore, Mythology and Legend*. New York: Funk & Wagnalls, 1972.

Mercatante, Anthony S. *The Facts on File Encyclopedia of World Mythology and Legend*. New York: Facts on File, 1988.

———. *Zoo of the Gods: Animals in Myth, Legend and Fable*. New York: Harper & Row Publishers, 1974.

New Shorter Oxford English Dictionary. Oxford: Clarendon Press, 1993.

Page, Michael. *The Encyclopedia of Things That Never Were: Creatures, Places, and People*. New York: Viking, 1987.

Pliny, Translated by H. Rackham. *Natural History* Volume 3, Books VIII–XI (Second Edition). Cambridge, MA: Harvard University Press, 1983.

Raffel, Burton, trans. *Beowulf*. New York: New American Library, 1963.

Rowland, Beryl. *Animals with Human Faces: A Guide to Animal Symbolism*. Knoxville, TN: The University of Tennessee Press, 1973.

South, Malcolm, ed. *Mythical and Fabulous Creatures: A Sourcebook and Research Guide*. New York: Greenwood Press, 1987.

White, T. H., trans. *The Book of Beasts, Being a Translation from a Latin Bestiary of the Twelfth Century*. New York: Dover Publications, Inc., 1984.

*I would like to thank the following people for their generous assistance
in the preparation of this book: Robert Longsworth, who scoured the
original manuscript for inconsistencies and offered his expert opinion on etymology
and spelling; Brian Sietsema, Ph.D., who graciously supplied the pronunciation key
for the beasts' names; Amy West, who pointed me in the right direction
when I had no idea how to pronounce "ichneumon"; and last but not least,
my editors Virginia Duncan, who has been stuck with me since* Illuminations,
*and Sarah Thomson, whose insights (and silly doodles)
kept me going when the going got tough.*

SIMON & SCHUSTER BOOKS FOR YOUNG READERS An imprint of Simon & Schuster Children's Publishing Division 1230 Avenue of the Americas, New York, New York 10020

Copyright © 1998 by Jonathan Hunt. All rights reserved including the right of reproduction in whole or in part in any form. SIMON & SCHUSTER BOOKS FOR YOUNG READERS is a trademark of Simon & Schuster.

Book design by Anahid Hamparian. The text of this book is set in 15-point Weideman. Printed in Hong Kong.

First Edition. 10 9 8 7 6 5 4 3 2 1

Library of Congress Cataloging-in-Publication Data. Hunt, Jonathan. Bestiary : a book of twenty-six fabulous beasts / by Jonathan Hunt.

p   cm.

Includes bibliographical references. Summary: An alphabet bestiary featuring mythical animals such as the amphisbaena, basilisk, and catoblepas.

ISBN 0-689-81246-9 1. Bestiaries—Juvenile literature. 2. Animals, Mythical—Juvenile literature. [1. Bestiaries. 2. Animals, Mythical. 3. Alphabet.] I. Title.

GR825.F45 1996

398.24'54—dc20 96-42102